THE GRAPHIC NOVELS SERIES

THE MAYOR OF CASTERBRIDGE

Published by
Evans Brothers Limited
2A Portman Mansions
Chiltern Street
London W1U 6NR

© in the modern text Hilary Burningham 2003
© in the illustrations Evans Brothers Ltd 2003
Designed by Design Systems Ltd

British Library Cataloguing in Publication Data
The Mayor of Casterbridge - (Graphic nevels)
1. Mayors - England - Wessex - Juvenile fiction
2. Wessex (England) - Social conditions - 19th century - Juvenile fiction
3. Children's stories
I. Title II. Hardy, Thomas, 1840-1928 III. Reed, Neil

ISBN 0 237 523140

Printed in Malta by Gutenberg Press Ltd.

*The symbol shown above and used throughout this book is a wyvern – a winged,
two-legged dragon. This symbol was used on shields and flags to represent the old
county of Wessex, which no longer exists. Thomas Hardy set many of his novels in
Wessex, reviving its name. Hardy's Wessex is entirely fictional.*

THE GRAPHIC NOVELS SERIES

THE MAYOR OF CASTERBRIDGE

THOMAS HARDY

RETOLD BY HILARY BURNINGHAM
ILLUSTRATED BY NEIL REED

Evans

EVANS BROTHERS LIMITED

It was Fair Day at Weydon Priors. A young man, his wife and their little girl had been walking all day. They went to the furmity tent for something to eat. Furmity was like porridge, with corn, flour, milk, raisins and currants all cooked together.

The woman selling the furmity put some rum in the man's bowl. He liked that. He kept asking for more furmity, more rum. The man, whose name was Michael, was drunk.

He began to play a silly game. He said that he wanted to sell his wife, Susan, and their daughter, Elizabeth-Jane.

A sailor paid him five guineas[1]. This was no longer a game. Michael took the money. Susan told him that she would go with the sailor.

The sailor spoke kindly to Susan. She took off her wedding ring and threw it at Michael. Then, sobbing, with the sailor on one arm and Elizabeth-Jane on the other, she left the tent. All the people were very quiet. They had never seen such a thing before.

Michael was left alone. He fell into a drunken sleep.

[1] five guineas – about five pounds and 25p

'Before you go further, Michael, listen to me. If you touch
that money, I and this girl go with the man. Mind, it is a joke
no longer.'

(Susan Henchard, Chapter 1)

Michael Henchard woke the next morning. He was alone. What had he done? Then he remembered. While drunk, he had sold his wife, Susan, and little Elizabeth-Jane.

He knew he had to find them, but first there was something he must do. He went to the church and swore an oath[1]. He swore that he would not touch alcohol for twenty-one years. It was alcohol that had made him do such a terrible thing. He chose twenty-one years because he was twenty-one years old: one year without alcohol for each year that he had lived.

Then he began to look for his wife and Elizabeth-Jane. Soon, the five guineas were all spent, paying for his search. At last, at a sea port, he heard of a family that sounded like the sailor, Susan and Elizabeth-Jane. They had emigrated[2].

He gave up his search and went to a town called Casterbridge in a far corner of Wessex.

---

[1] swore an oath – made a solemn promise to God
[2] emigrated – gone to live in one of the 'new countries' abroad: Canada, Australia and South Africa

'I, Michael Henchard, on this morning of the sixteenth of September, do take an oath before God here in this solemn place that I will avoid all strong liquors for the space of twenty-one years to come, being a year for every year that I have lived.'

(Chapter 2)

Many years had passed. Susan Henchard was now called Susan Newson. Although they were not married, she had taken the sailor's last name. Elizabeth-Jane was a young woman, eighteen years old. The sailor, Richard Newson, had been lost at sea. They thought that he was dead. Susan had returned to Weydon Priors to look for Michael Henchard, her real husband.

Elizabeth-Jane had no idea that her mother was married to Henchard. Susan told her only that he was related to them by marriage. That was not a lie, but it was not the whole truth.

It was fair day again in Weydon Priors. The same furmity woman was there. Susan spoke to her. The woman remembered the man who had sold his wife and daughter. He had returned a year later and left instructions. If anyone came looking for him, he said, she was to say that he had gone to Casterbridge.

'The only reason why I can mind the man is that he came back here to the next year's fair, and told me quite private-like that if a woman ever asked for him I was to say he had gone to – where? – Casterbridge – yes – to Casterbridge, said he.'

(Mrs Goodenough, the furmity woman, Chapter 3)

The next day, Susan and Elizabeth-Jane arrived at Casterbridge. People were complaining about the bread. There was no good bread in town. The town corn-merchant had sold bad wheat to all the bakers. The bread had made people ill.

At the King's Arms, the main hotel in Casterbridge, a great public dinner was taking place. The most important person there was the mayor. Through the window, Susan and Elizabeth-Jane could see the mayor sitting at the head of the table. Susan recognised him at once. He was Michael Henchard.

Around them, people were saying that it was Henchard who was selling the bad wheat.

'Why, my good maid, he's the powerfullest member of the Town Council, and quite a principal man in the country round besides. Never a big dealing in wheat, barley, oats, hay, roots, and such-like but Henchard's got a hand in it.'

(Christopher Coney, an onlooker, speaking to Elizabeth-Jane, Chapter 5)

There was a young Scotchman also looking through the window with the others. He walked to the door and asked a waiter to pass a note to Henchard. When Henchard was given the note, he appeared to be thinking very hard.

The Scotchman was looking for a place to stay. The waiter said that the Three Mariners was not too expensive.

The Scotchman went to the Three Mariners. Susan and Elizabeth-Jane decided to stay there, too.

The waiter took the note, while the young stranger continued –
'And can ye tell me of a respectable hotel that's a little more
moderate than this?'

(Donald Farfrae, Chapter 6)

At the Three Mariners, Susan and Elizabeth-Jane's room was next door to that of the Scotchman.

Michael Henchard came to see him. The two rooms had once had a connecting door, which was now nailed shut and papered over. Through the hidden door, Susan and Elizabeth-Jane could hear every word that was said.

The Scotchman, whose name was Donald Farfrae, knew of a way to make Henchard's bad wheat good. Henchard was very pleased. If he could make the wheat fit to eat, he could sell it instead of throwing it away. He offered Farfrae money in payment for his advice, but Farfrae refused to take it.

Henchard could see that Farfrae was a good man. He asked him to become his manager at his corn yard. Farfrae refused. He was planning to go to America.

Henchard tried very hard to persuade Farfrae to stay, but his mind was made up.

'Have you really made up your mind about this American
notion? I won't mince matters. I feel you would be invaluable
to me – that needn't be said – and if you will bide and be my
manager I will make it worth your while.'

(Michael Henchard, Chapter 7)

15

Later, Donald Farfrae went down to the main room of the inn. People there often sang together in the evenings.

Farfrae was a very good singer. He sang a sad, beautiful song about Scotland. Elizabeth-Jane stood by quietly and listened. She loved music.

Farfrae was very popular at the Three Mariners. The people there wanted him to stay in Casterbridge.

Outside in the street, Henchard listened and thought. He, too, wanted Farfrae to stay in Casterbridge.

'It's hame, and it's hame, hame fain would I be, O hame, hame, hame to my ain countree!'

(Donald Farfrae, Chapter 8)

The next day, Susan sent Elizabeth-Jane to Henchard with a message. Elizabeth-Jane was to say that his relative, Susan, a sailor's widow, was in the town. If he wanted to see her, he was to send a note saying where and when.

When Elizabeth-Jane arrived at Henchard's office, she got a surprise. Farfrae was there. He had decided to stay and work for Henchard, after all.

Elizabeth turned the handle; and there stood before her, bending over some sample-bags on a table, not the corn merchant but the young Scotchman, Mr Farfrae – in the act of pouring some grains of wheat from one hand to the other.

(Chapter 9)

Elizabeth-Jane sat waiting to see Henchard.
Suddenly, another man pushed his way into
Henchard's office. His name was Joshua Jopp.
He had expected to be Henchard's new manager.
Jopp was very angry not to get the job.

She could see that his mouth twitched with anger, and that
bitter disappointment was written in his face everywhere.

(Chapter 10)

At last, Elizabeth-Jane was able to see Henchard.
She gave him the message about Susan, the sailor's
widow. Henchard was very surprised by the message.

Henchard was gentle and kind, asking Elizabeth-
Jane a lot of questions. From her answers he realised
that Susan had not told Elizabeth-Jane who he was.
His dreadful secret, that he had sold his own wife
and daughter, was still safe. He gave Elizabeth-Jane
a note for Susan. He put some money in the note:
exactly five guineas.

Later that day, Susan met Henchard at a place called
The Ring. Michael Henchard held his wife in his
arms. He had found her again, and his daughter,
Elizabeth-Jane.

Henchard needed a plan. He was now a respectable
man, the mayor of Casterbridge. No one knew he
had once been married, with a daughter. He decided
to be careful. Susan and Elizabeth-Jane would rent
a cottage in the town. He would call on them.
After a while, he and Susan would 'marry' again.
Everyone would think that Elizabeth-Jane was his
'step-daughter'. Only he and Susan would know
that he had his wife and daughter back.

'I don't drink,' he said in a low, halting, apologetic voice. 'You hear, Susan? – I don't drink now – I haven't since that night.' Those were his first words.

(Michael Henchard, Chapter 11)

That night, Henchard told his new friend, Farfrae, a story. It was the story of Susan and Elizabeth-Jane: how, while drunk, he had sold them to a sailor for five guineas. How he had sworn not to drink for twenty-one years. How he had tried to find them again. How, this very day, Susan and his daughter had returned.

But there was a problem. In the meantime, Henchard had met another young lady in Jersey. He went often to Jersey on business. On one of his business trips he had fallen ill. The young lady had looked after him. There had been a lot of gossip about them in Jersey. Thinking Susan dead, he had promised to marry the young lady.

Henchard knew that he had to be with Susan and Elizabeth-Jane, but he wanted to be kind to the lady in Jersey. He asked Farfrae to help him write a letter to her, explaining that Susan was alive. He was not free to marry her as he thought.

Farfrae wrote the letter, which Henchard copied in his own handwriting. He sent the letter, and some money, to the young lady in Jersey.

'But, being together in the same house, and her feelings warm, we got naturally intimate. I won't go into particulars of what our relations were. It is enough to say that we honestly meant to marry. There arose a scandal, which did me no harm, but was of course ruin to her.'

(Michael Henchard, Chapter 12)

As Henchard had planned, he rented a cottage for Susan and Elizabeth-Jane. He called upon them regularly and, after a time, he and Susan were married – again.

Susan and Elizabeth-Jane moved into Henchard's big house. Everyone believed that Elizabeth-Jane was Henchard's step-daughter. Elizabeth-Jane could now afford to buy nice clothes. She began to look very pretty.

One day, she and Donald Farfrae were tricked into meeting together at a granary where Henchard was doing business. They had each been sent an anonymous[1] note. They met and talked. Although they liked each other, it was very mysterious. Who had arranged their meeting?

[1] anonymous – sent by someone unknown

'Didn't you ask me to come here? Didn't you write this?'
Elizabeth held out her note.
'No. Indeed at no hand would I have thought of it. And for
you – didn't you ask me? This is not your writing?' And he
held up his.

(Elizabeth-Jane and Donald Farfrae, Chapter 14)

Farfrae soon began to be more popular in the town than Henchard. Henchard was becoming jealous. He was sorry that he had told Farfrae his secrets.

One day there was a celebration in the town. Henchard spent a lot of money on games and prizes. He put out tables with lots of food. It rained that day, and his games and food were ruined. No one came. Disappointed, he went to see where all the people were.

In another part of the town, Farfrae was also having a party. He strung cloths between the trees to make a big tent, where he had highland dancing. All the people went there because it was raining. When Henchard arrived, everyone was having a wonderful time. They were all talking about Farfrae. They thought that he was very clever. Some even said he was better than Henchard.

Henchard was angry. He thought that Farfrae had deliberately planned to make his party better. In a rage he said, in front of everyone, that Farfrae was leaving as his manager. Farfrae quietly agreed. The next day, Henchard knew that he had made a terrible mistake. But this time, Farfrae would not change his mind.

'Mr Henchard's rejoicings couldn't say good morning to this,'
said one. 'A man must be a headstrong stunpoll to think folk
would go up to that bleak place today.'

(An onlooker, praising Donald Farfrae's plan, Chapter 16)

Elizabeth-Jane and Farfrae were becoming close
friends. They often went out walking together.
Sometimes it almost seemed as if they were falling
in love.

After Henchard fired him, Farfrae set up his own
business. Henchard told Elizabeth-Jane not to see
Farfrae any more. He wrote to Farfrae, telling him
not to see Elizabeth-Jane. Although Farfrae liked
Elizabeth-Jane, he agreed to do as Henchard said.

One day, Henchard received a note from Lucetta,
the lady in Jersey. She would be passing through
Casterbridge. She asked Henchard to give back all
the letters she had written to him after he left Jersey.
She asked him to meet the coach when it changed
horses at Casterbridge. Henchard met the coach but
there was no Lucetta. He still had her letters.

The evening was chilly, and the coach was late. Henchard crossed over to it while the horses were being changed; but there was no Lucetta inside or out.

(Chapter 18)

Not long after her marriage, Susan Henchard became seriously ill. Knowing she was dying, she wrote a note to Henchard and addressed it: *Mr Michael Henchard. Not to be opened till Elizabeth-Jane's wedding day.*

Elizabeth-Jane sat with her dying mother. Susan talked about Elizabeth-Jane's meeting with Farfrae at the granary. Susan admitted that she had sent the messages to them both. She liked Farfrae and was trying to bring them together.

Soon afterwards, Susan Henchard died. Elizabeth-Jane had always thought that Richard Newson, the sailor, was her father. Now Henchard told her that he was her real father. He wanted her to have his name. Looking for papers to prove to Elizabeth-Jane that he was her father, he found Susan's letter, *'Not to be opened till Elizabeth-Jane's wedding day'*. It was not properly closed. Henchard read it.

To Henchard's horror, Susan had written that his real daughter, Elizabeth-Jane, had died three months after they had parted at the furmity tent. Later, Susan had had a child with Richard Newson. This was the Elizabeth-Jane she had brought to Casterbridge. Henchard was bitterly disappointed, but decided not to tell Elizabeth-Jane the truth. He wanted her to continue to think that she was his daughter.

'And I am going to look upon you as the father that you are, and not to call you Mr Henchard any more. It is so plain to me now – indeed, Father, it is; for of course you would not have done half the things you have done for me, and let me have my own way so entirely, and bought me presents, if I had only been your step-daughter.'

(Elizabeth-Jane, Chapter 19)

Elizabeth-Jane was ready to call Henchard, 'Father', but his feelings had changed now that he knew she was Newson's child, not his.

He criticised everything about her: the way she spoke, the way she treated the servants, even her handwriting. The criticism made Elizabeth-Jane very unhappy. She tried hard to please him, but could not understand why he always seemed so cross and bad-tempered.

One day, visiting her mother's grave, Elizabeth-Jane met a pleasant and friendly young woman. She wore a veil but Elizabeth-Jane could see that she was very pretty. The woman was going to live in Casterbridge. She guessed that Elizabeth-Jane was unhappy. She suggested that Elizabeth-Jane live in her house as a housekeeper-companion. Elizabeth was delighted at the thought of getting away from Henchard.

'Now what do you think of this – I shall soon want somebody to live in my house – partly as housekeeper, partly as companion – would you mind coming to me?'

(Young woman speaking to Elizabeth-Jane, Chapter 20)

Elizabeth-Jane told Henchard that she had a chance to move to a different household. He seemed not to care, though he arranged a small annuity[1] for her.

By six o'clock that day Elizabeth-Jane was putting her boxes and bags into a carriage. Henchard had not expected her to move out so soon. Going up to her room, he saw how she had tried to improve herself by reading books, practising her writing, and arranging everything nicely. He suddenly realised that she had been trying to please him. He rushed back to the carriage and begged her not to go, but it was too late. She had made up her mind. She was moving to High-Place Hall.

The evening before, Henchard had received a letter from Lucetta, the lady from Jersey. A relative had died, leaving her some money. She had decided to live in Casterbridge, to be near Henchard.

After Elizabeth-Jane moved out, Henchard received another letter from Lucetta. She was living at High-Place Hall, and Elizabeth-Jane was to be her companion. Henchard would have a good excuse for calling at High-Place Hall: to visit Elizabeth-Jane. Henchard was pleased. He thought Lucetta had been rather clever.

[1] a small annuity – a small amount of money paid every year

'The artful little woman!' he said smiling (with reference to Lucetta's adroit and pleasant manoeuvre with Elizabeth-Jane).

(Michael Henchard, Chapter 22)

Lucetta now waited for Henchard to call upon her.
When he did not call, she thought he might be
avoiding Elizabeth-Jane. One morning, she sent
Elizabeth-Jane on some errands and sent Henchard
a note, asking him to visit her; she would be alone.

A man did come to see her, but it was not Henchard.
It was Farfrae, hoping to see Elizabeth-Jane. Lucetta
and Farfrae talked together. They liked each other
very much. There was a strong feeling between
them. Farfrae forgot that he had come to see
Elizabeth-Jane. Lucetta forgot that she had been
waiting for Henchard. They agreed to meet again.

Later, when Henchard finally came, Lucetta did not
want to see him. Her maid sent him away. Lucetta
was thinking about Farfrae.

'I'll come another time – if I may, ma'am?'
'Certainly,' she said. 'What has happened to us today is very curious.'
'Something to think over when we are alone, it's like to be.'

(Donald Farfrae and Lucetta, Chapter 23)

One day, a new piece of machinery was brought to Casterbridge. It was a seed-drill, for sowing seeds. Farmers could use it to sow their seeds more quickly. They would not waste so many.

Henchard made fun of the seed-drill. Farfrae said it was a very good thing for the farmers.

Lucetta and Farfrae were falling in love. Lucetta now liked Farfrae much better than Henchard. But she had met Henchard first, in Jersey. She had come to Casterbridge because she thought she wanted to marry him. What should she do?

She told Elizabeth-Jane her story, as if it had happened to a friend. Elizabeth-Jane knew that Lucetta was talking about herself, but who were the two men in the story?

'Stupid? Oh, no!' said Farfrae gravely. 'It will revolutionise sowing hereabout. No more sowers flinging their seed about broadcast, so that some falls by the wayside, and some among thorns, and all that. Each grain will go straight to its intended place, and nowhere else whatever!'

(Donald Farfrae, Chapter 24)

After Susan's death, Henchard had waited some time before trying to see Lucetta. When they met in the marketplace, her feelings for him had begun to cool.

Soon after, he called on her and asked her to marry him. He reminded her that many people in Jersey knew about their affair. People in Casterbridge might find out, too. Lucetta asked for more time. Henchard became angry. Lucetta had come to Casterbridge to be near him, but now she did not seem to want to accept his offer of marriage.

Elizabeth-Jane could see what was happening. She was sad that both Henchard and Farfrae, being more interested in Lucetta, completely ignored her. She still believed Henchard to be her father. How could he have changed so much towards her?

One day Henchard came to tea. By coincidence, Farfrae came at the same time. Although Lucetta tried to hide her feelings, she paid more attention to Farfrae. Henchard went away disappointed. Elizabeth-Jane could see that Lucetta and Farfrae were in love.

Henchard took a slice [of bread] by one end and Donald by the other; each feeling certain he was the man meant, neither let go, and the slice came in two.

(Chapter 26)

Henchard had got rid of Farfrae as his foreman. Realising that he needed a new foreman, he hired Joshua Jopp.

Years before, Jopp had lived in Jersey. He had heard the gossip and knew about Henchard and Lucetta. Up to now, Jopp had not told anyone in Casterbridge about what he knew.

Henchard was still the biggest corn and hay dealer in the town, but Farfrae was taking a lot of his trade. People liked and trusted him. Jopp was one person who didn't like Farfrae, because he had taken the manager's job with Henchard. Henchard planned with Jopp how they could get rid of the Scotchman.

'The Scotchman who's taking the town trade so bold into his hands must be cut out. D'ye hear? We two can't live side by side – that's clear and certain.'

(Michael Henchard, Chapter 26)

Corn dealers had to know when to buy, how much to pay, and when to sell their corn. Henchard had to buy at a low price and sell at a higher price. That was how he made a profit.

The weather forecasts were not good that year. Henchard bought a lot of wheat at high prices. The weather got much better, there was a good harvest, and prices went down. Henchard had to sell at a low price and lost a great deal of money. Instead of blaming himself, he blamed Jopp and fired him.

It was the second time he had treated Jopp badly. Jopp swore that he would make Henchard sorry one day.

'You shall be sorry for this sir; sorry as a man can be!' said Jopp, standing pale, and looking after the corn-merchant as he disappeared in the crowd of market-men hard by.

(Chapter 26)

Unlike Henchard, Farfrae waited to see if the weather forecasts were correct, then bought his corn when the price was low. He sold it when the price went up and made a good profit. Henchard had another reason to dislike him. He was jealous of his good fortune.

One night, Henchard saw Lucetta and Farfrae out walking. To avoid meeting them, he hid nearby. From his hiding-place he could hear their conversation. It was obvious that they were in love and planning to marry.

Henchard went mad with jealousy. He followed Lucetta home and burst in on her. She was terrified. Henchard said that she had to promise to marry him. If she refused, he would tell everyone that they had been lovers in Jersey. There would be a scandal.

Elizabeth-Jane was called from her room. In front of her, Lucetta agreed to marry Henchard. Elizabeth-Jane could see that Lucetta was very unhappy but didn't know why. She didn't know that Henchard was forcing her to marry him.

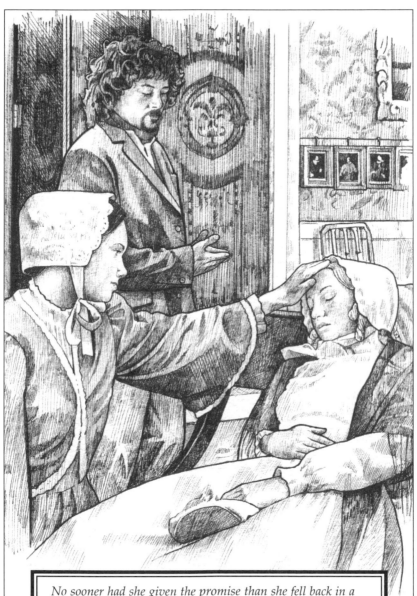

No sooner had she given the promise than she fell back in a
fainting state.
'What dreadful thing drives her to say this, Father, when
it is such a pain to her?' asked Elizabeth, kneeling down
by Lucetta.

(Chapter 27)

Michael Henchard was no longer the mayor of Casterbridge. His term had ended. He was also no longer a member of the Town Council, having been replaced by Farfrae. He was, however, still a Justice of the Peace[1] and went the next morning to the Town Hall to hear a case in court. There was only one case: an old woman who had been a nuisance. She reminded Henchard of someone but he couldn't think who it might be.

The woman looked hard at Henchard and began to speak. She told a strange story. Twenty years before, she was selling furmity at Weydon Fair. She told how a man had sold his wife and child to a sailor, for five guineas. That man, she said, was one of the magistrates in court that day. She pointed to Henchard.

Everyone heard her. Henchard said that her story was true, and left the court. Soon everyone in the town would hear the story. They would all know the secret he had kept for so many years.

---

[1] Justice of the Peace – a magistrate, a type of unpaid judge, appointed to help keep order in a town and hear some cases in court

'A sailor came in, and bid five guineas, and paid the money, and led her away. And the man who sold his wife in that fashion is the man sitting there in the great big chair.'

(The furmity woman, pointing at Henchard, Chapter 28)

When Lucetta heard the story, she was very frightened. This was the man who had made her promise to marry him. She went away for a few days.

When Lucetta returned, Elizabeth-Jane went out to meet her on a country road. They were chased by an angry bull. Henchard saved them. He wanted to talk to Lucetta.

Henchard owed a lot of money. If it was known that he was to marry Lucetta, a rich woman, his creditors[1] would wait. For just two weeks, he wanted to be able to say that they were going to be married. Desperately, Lucetta told him she could not help him. Mr Grower, the man to whom Henchard owed the most money, had been a witness at her wedding – her wedding to Donald Farfrae.

Henchard was shocked. Lucetta had promised to marry him, then had gone away and married Farfrae. Lucetta reminded him that he had threatened to tell Farfrae about their affair in Jersey. When she had heard how he had sold his wife and daughter at a fair as if they had been animals, she had been frightened. She had gone away and married Farfrae.

Henchard was furious.

[1] creditors – people to whom someone owes money

'And then, when I had promised you, I learnt of the rumour that you had – sold your first wife at a fair, like a horse or cow. How could I keep my promise after hearing that? – I could not risk myself in your hands.'

(Lucetta, Chapter 29)

The church bells were ringing for Lucetta and
Farfrae. Lucetta told Elizabeth-Jane about their
marriage. Farfrae was moving into High-Place Hall.

Elizabeth-Jane did not agree with the marriage.
She still loved her father and thought that Lucetta
should have married him, as she had promised,
or no one at all. Also, she had almost fallen in love
with Farfrae herself. She was not happy staying in
the house any longer. That night, she moved to a
small lodging near Henchard's house.

From the time that the furmity woman told his
secret, everything went wrong for Henchard.
He owed a lot of money. He could not pay his bills.
He became bankrupt[1].

Henchard moved out of his big house and took a
couple of rooms in the cottage of his old enemy,
Jopp. All his furniture was sold. Even his grain yard
was bought by Donald Farfrae.

---

[1] bankrupt – having to sell everything one owns to pay off debts

'Mr Farfrae is master here?'
'Yaas, Miss Henchet,' he said, 'Mr Farfrae have bought the concern and all of we work-folk with it; and 'tis better for us than 'twas —'

(Elizabeth-Jane and a worker at the grain yard, Chapter 31)

Farfrae tried to help Henchard whenever he could. He bought Henchard's large house and offered to let him stay there. He told Henchard to choose whatever furniture he would like to have from his former home. Henchard refused his offers of help.

Henchard got a job in Farfrae's yard. He was following his former trade – trussing hay[1]. He was almost beginning to like Farfrae when he heard that Farfrae might become mayor. Henchard's jealousy returned. Farfrae had the big house, he had Lucetta, and now he was to become mayor. It was too much for Henchard.

The twenty-one years had passed since Henchard swore his oath not to touch alcohol. He went to the Three Mariners and got very drunk. He sang. He shouted. He threatened his friends with a poker.

Hearing what was happening, Elizabeth-Jane came and took him home. Henchard was a violent man when he was drunk. Elizabeth-Jane began to worry – he hated Farfrae so much that he might do him harm.

---

[1] trussing hay – tying hay into neat bundles after it has been cut

He slipped off the table, seized the poker, and going to the door placed his back against it.

(Chapter 33)

Lucetta was still trying to get back the letters she had
written Henchard from Jersey. Henchard remembered
that he had left them in the wall safe in the big house
where Farfrae and Lucetta were now living. One
evening, he collected the letters and took them home.

The next day, Lucetta met Henchard and begged
him for her letters. He felt sorry for her and agreed
to return them. When she got home, Lucetta found
Jopp waiting at her door. He wanted her to help him
get a job at Farfrae's. She refused, making him angry.

That night, Henchard put the letters in a sealed
packet and gave it to Jopp to give to Mrs Farfrae.
Jopp was angry with her because she had refused to
help him. He was also angry with Henchard, who
had fired him. He took the letters to a pub called
Peter's Finger on Mixen Lane. The people there
were very rough. They didn't like people like Mrs
Farfrae. Jopp read aloud Lucetta's love-letters. The
people in the pub began talking about something
called a 'skimmity-ride'.

The next morning, Jopp at last took the letters to
Lucetta. She burned them immediately. But now a
lot of people knew about them.

'Mrs Farfrae wrote that!' said Nance Mockridge. ''Tis a humbling thing for us, as respectable women, that one of the same sex could do it. And now she's vowed herself to another man!'

(Chapter 36)

There was great excitement in Casterbridge. A royal visitor was coming to the town. The mayor, Donald Farfrae, and the Council had a meeting to plan the welcome ceremony. Henchard interrupted the meeting. He wanted to welcome the visitor, too. Farfrae and the Council refused. Henchard was no longer the mayor or even a member of the Council.

On the day of the visit, Donald Farfrae in his Chain of Office, and the Council, all in their best robes, officially welcomed the royal visitor. Lucetta and the other ladies wore their best clothes.

Michael Henchard refused to be left out. He had planned his own welcome. His clothes by now were very shabby, and he carried a home-made flag. He had drunk a large glass of rum and was determined to shake hands with the royal visitor. Farfrae dragged him back and told him to go away. Henchard grew even more angry towards Farfrae.

Some of the Mixen Lane folk were standing nearby. They all knew about Lucetta and Michael Henchard. The plans for the skimmity-ride were going ahead.

He had unrolled his private flag, and removing his hat he staggered to the side of the slowing vehicle, waving the Union Jack to and fro with his left hand, while he blandly held out his right to the illustrious personage.

(Chapter 37)

Henchard thought about how Farfrae had pushed him aside at the royal visit. He became more and more angry. He decided to fight Farfrae.

He left a message at Farfrae's house to meet him at the granaries. While waiting for Farfrae, he tied his arm at his side. He was bigger and stronger than Farfrae. This would make the fight more even. He waited in the loft.

Farfrae arrived. He had no idea what Henchard wanted. He climbed up to the loft and Henchard attacked him. The two men fought. Henchard was detemined to push Farfrae out of the loft door. Henchard got Farfrae in his power, with Farfrae's head hanging out of the loft, high above the ground. At the last moment, as he looked down at the man who had once been his friend, Henchard could not kill him. He told Farfrae to leave.

Farfrae got his horse and carriage. He had business to do. Henchard felt he wanted to talk to Farfrae again, but knew that he wouldn't be home until late.

In the distance, Henchard could hear strange noises: shouting and voices raised.

'And now – though I came here to kill 'ee, I cannot hurt thee! Go and give me in charge – do what you will – I care nothing for what comes of me!'

(Michael Henchard, Chapter 38)

It was time for the skimmity-ride. The people of Mixen had made dummies: life-like models of Lucetta and Henchard. The models were tied on to a horse, back to back, and sent riding round the town. A rough crowd followed them, shouting and laughing.

Farfrae had received an anonymous message earlier sending him out of town. Some people did not want him to see the skimmity-ride. They only wanted to hurt Lucetta and Henchard.

Lucetta was alone, waiting for Farfrae to come home. She heard a noise in the street. Suddenly, Elizabeth-Jane rushed in and tried to close the shutters. She didn't want Lucetta to see the skimmity-ride, but she was too late. Lucetta saw the two images, dressed like herself and Henchard, being paraded around the town. The whole town knew about their affair. She shrieked and fainted, then fell to the ground.

'She's me – she's me – even to the parasol – my green parasol!'
cried Lucetta with a wild laugh as she stepped in. She stood
motionless for one second – then fell heavily to the floor.

(Lucetta, Chapter 39)

Henchard saw the skimmity-ride and knew what it meant. He went straight to the Farfraes'. Lucetta was very ill. The doctor wanted Farfrae home at once.

Everyone thought Farfrae had gone to Budmouth. But Henchard had overheard a conversation in the granary and knew that Farfrae had gone to Mellstock and Weatherbury. He tried to tell them, but no one would believe him. After the royal visit, everyone thought he was mad.

Henchard set out to find Farfrae himself. He met him on the road, but Farfrae did not believe his story, either. Since the fight in the granary, Farfrae didn't trust him. To Henchard's despair, Farfrae continued on to Mellstock. The journey would take at least two hours.

By the time Farfrae returned home, Lucetta was dying. She was pregnant, and the shock of the skimmity-ride had been too much.

A cloth had been wrapped around the door-knocker at the Farfraes' house, so as not to disturb Lucetta. When Henchard came along very early the next morning, a servant was removing it. There was no need to be quiet. Lucetta was dead.

She turned in some surprise at his presence, and did not answer for an instant or two. Recognising him she said, 'Because they may knock as loud as they will: she will never hear it any more.'

(Servant speaking to Michael Henchard, Chapter 40)

The next day, exhausted, Elizabeth-Jane went to see Henchard and to tell him that Lucetta was dead. To her surprise, he seemed pleased to see her. He told her to lie down in the next room while he made some breakfast. In fact, Henchard's feelings towards Elizabeth-Jane had changed yet again. He was beginning to hope that she would come back to him as his daughter.

There was a knock on the door. It was Richard Newson, Elizabeth-Jane's real father. Henchard told him Susan was dead. When Newson asked about Elizabeth-Jane, who was asleep in the next room, he found himself saying that she was dead, too. Newson left, sad and disappointed.

Henchard realised how lonely he had been and how much he loved Elizabeth-Jane. But having lied to Newson, he would always be afraid that Newson would find out the truth and come back for his daughter.

In spite of everything, Farfrae still wanted to help Henchard. The Town Council, led by Farfrae, bought him a small business. It was a small seed and root store, and he and Elizabeth-Jane lived quietly over the shop.

'They told me in Falmouth that Susan was dead. But my
Elizabeth-Jane – where is she?'
'Dead likewise,' said Henchard doggedly. 'Surely you learnt
that, too?'

(Richard Newson and Michael Henchard, Chapter 41)

After a time, Farfrae and Elizabeth-Jane began seeing each other again. Henchard was very worried. He did not want to lose her.

One day, Henchard was watching the Budmouth Road, where Farfrae and Elizabeth-Jane often walked together. He saw a man coming towards him. It was Newson. Henchard knew he had learned the truth about Elizabeth-Jane. It was only a matter of time until they were re-united.

Henchard went home and talked with Elizabeth-Jane. Without giving the real reason, he said he was leaving Casterbridge. She was very upset. She and Farfrae were hoping to be married. Henchard would not be at their wedding.

That night, Henchard left Casterbridge. Elizabeth-Jane walked with him a short distance, then they said goodbye. He knew, though she didn't, that her real father was waiting for her. Henchard had committed many sins in his life, especially lying to Newson. Now he had to accept the loneliness as his punishment.

With Farfrae, Elizabeth-Jane met her father, Richard Newson, again. It was a very happy meeting. Together, the three of them began to plan the wedding.

'Well, well – never mind – it is all over and past,' said Newson good-naturedly. 'Now, about this wedding again.'

(Chapter 44)

Lonely and miserable, Henchard worked around the countryside. From some passing travellers, he learned the date of Elizabeth-Jane's wedding. He began to wonder if Elizabeth-Jane wanted him to be there. He decided to go.

Henchard bought some new clothes: a new coat and hat, a new shirt and neck-cloth. The clothes were rough, but clean. He bought a gift: a goldfinch in a little cage. Carrying his gift, and wearing his new clothes, he arrived at the wedding.

While he waited in a small side-room to speak to Elizabeth-Jane, he watched the wedding guests through the open door. Newson was there, dancing with the other guests. He could see Elizabeth-Jane, wearing a beautiful white wedding dress. They all seemed very happy, and he was not a part of it.

Elizabeth-Jane was surprised to see him. She was still very angry about the way he had lied to Newson. She spoke harshly, saying she could not love or forgive him. Henchard, though he was hurt, said proudly that he would not trouble her again. Forgetting about his gift, he went on his way.

'I have done wrong in coming to 'ee. I see my error; but it is only for once, so forgive it. I'll never trouble 'ee again, Elizabeth-Jane – no, not to my dying day. Good-night. Good-bye!'

(Michael Henchard, Chapter 44)

Some days later, Elizabeth-Jane found the birdcage and the dead bird – Henchard's wedding gift. She began to feel sorry for sending him away, and asked Farfrae to help her find him.

Elizabeth-Jane and Farfrae found Henchard at last, at the cottage of a man named Whittle. He had once worked for Henchard. Although Henchard had not been kind to Whittle, he had helped Whittle's mother in many small ways. Whittle had looked after him. Whittle told Elizabeth-Jane and Farfrae that Henchard had died just half an hour before. He never knew that Elizabeth-Jane had forgiven him and had searched for him.

Elizabeth-Jane was very sad for a long time after Henchard's death. She was sorry not to have seen him again and made her peace with him.

As time went on, she taught those around her some of the lessons that she had learned in her life: especially the importance of enjoying small pleasures. She also understood that her good fortune had come about by chance, and there were many equally deserving people who ended up with much less.

Her teaching had a reflex action upon herself, insomuch that she thought she could perceive no great personal difference between being respected in the nether parts of Casterbridge, and glorified at the uppermost end of the social world.

(Chapter 45)

*Also available in the
Graphic Novels Series:*

GREAT EXPECTATIONS
CHARLES DICKENS

Retold by Hilary Burningham

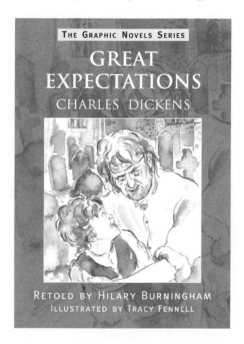

See over for details of our Graphic Shakespeare Series

*If you enjoyed reading this book,
you may wish to read other books in the
sister series:*

The Graphic Shakespeare Series

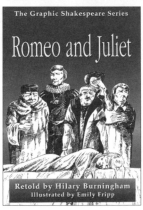

The titles in the Graphic Shakespeare Series
are an ideal introduction to Shakespeare's
plays, but can equally well be used
as revision aids.

The main characters and key events
are brought to life in the simplified story
and dramatic pictures, and the short extracts
from the original play focus on key speeches
in Shakespeare's language.

*Available in the
Graphic Shakespeare Series:*

**A Midsummer Night's Dream
Henry V
Julius Caesar
Macbeth
Romeo and Juliet
The Tempest
Twelfth Night**

EVANS BROTHERS LIMITED